The Adventures of Sam Pig

Sam Pig at the Theatre
Alison Uttley

Illustrated by Graham Percy

ff
faber and faber
LONDON · BOSTON

First published in 1940
by Faber and Faber Limited
3 Queen Square London WC1N 3AU
This edition first published in 1989

Phototypeset by Input Typesetting Ltd, London

Printed in Great Britain by
W. S. Cowell Ltd, Ipswich

A CIP record for this book is available from the British Library.

ISBN 0–571–15471–9

Holly

Sam Pig at the Theatre

'Have you ever been to a theatre, Badger?' asked
Sam Pig one day when the little family sat at dinner.

What a strange question to ask! Bill Pig stopped
with a roast potato half-way to his mouth, and Tom
Pig dropped his bread on the floor. Ann opened
wide her small blue eyes and gasped with astonish-
ment. What was brother Sam talking about now!

Only Brock the Badger took it calmly. Not one of his black-and-silver hairs quivered, not a muscle moved. He took up a piece of toast and dripping and had a bite before he answered the young pig.

'No,' he drawled. 'I can't say as I've ever been to a theatre, Sam.'

'But what is it? What is a theatre?' they all asked quickly.

'It's a play-acting house, where anyone pretends to be somebody else,' explained Sam, proud of his knowledge.

'Like the Wolf pretending to be a poor lone sheep?' asked Ann. 'I shouldn't like that at all.'

'Like the Fox pretending to be dead?' asked Bill.

'Like a falling leaf pretending to be a butterfly?' asked Tom.

'Well, something like those things,' said Sam. 'I've never actually been to a theatre, but I've been talking to Sally the mare, and she says there's a theatre on Midsummer Eve.'

'Where? Oh where?' they asked in a gabble of surprise.

'At the farm, in the stable or barn, I don't know exactly. We are all invited, and they asked me to take my fiddle,' said Sam.

'It's Midsummer Eve tomorrow,' said Badger. 'Well, I've never seen a theatre, so we will all go together, and see the fun, whatever it is.'

There were great preparations. Sam Pig had a bath in the wash-tub the night before, and on the morning of Midsummer Eve he scrubbed his face so that it shone like a lamp.

'If there wasn't a moon we could see by the light of your face,' said Bill.

Then Sam threw a clod of soil at Bill, and Bill tossed it back again, and Sam had to wash once more.

Tom got out his blacking-pot and the brushes and he polished everybody's hooves. Ann gave a twist and curl to all the little tails and she swept a little furze brush over the creamy hairs on her brothers' heads. Badger was very busy in his bedroom, making himself into a fine country gentleman. Bill brought buttonholes of moss roses and parsley for each of the pigs to wear. Tom gave out sticks of barley honey for each of them to suck. Barley honey is made out of honeycomb and ground barley, and very delicious it is.

Badger cut stout staffs to help them on the journey, and Sam as usual got in everybody's way as he ran here and there trying to help.

At last it was time to depart. The moon had risen and the stars were peeping through the soft clouds. A little breeze ruffled the leaves and the woods sang their evening hymn to the coming of night. The fields were silvery with dew, and a nightingale sang in the oak tree.

'Jug. Jug. Jug. Tirra la-a-a. How happy I am! Sweet. Sweet,' it sang and they all stood listening to its exquisite voice.

'We're going to a theatre. Tirra la-a-a,' piped Sam in his thinnest wee voice, as he tried to rival the bird.

'How happy I am! I have a mate and a nest with a brood of young ones,' sang the bird in rapture.

'Be quiet, Sam,' chided Brock. 'Animals are silent when they walk the woods by night. Only the nightingale and the owl may raise their voices. Come along softly and don't walk in the moon shadows, or the goblins will get you. They'll pull your tail and swing you on their backs and carry you off.'

Sam looked quickly behind him at the blue shadows. Then he saw that Badger was laughing

at him, so he pressed close to his friend and trotted quietly along.

When they arrived at the farm they tiptoed very gently over the lawn and round the flower-beds, for it would never do to leave a trail on the soil. The watch-dog lay in his kennel with one eye watching them. He gave no alarm, for of course he knew about the festivities. The farmhouse was in darkness with the shutters closed and never a glimmer of light showing. On Midsummer Eve it was considered dangerous to be abroad, for strange things happened.

The animals padded across the yard to the stable from which came a faint glow. They pushed their way through the little crowd in the doorway and gazed around in admiration.

The horses' stalls were festooned with green leaves, and from the roof hung a horn lantern with a light like a pale moon. The mangers were filled with forget-me-nots and the walls were decked with streamers of ivy. In the wallholes, where usually the horse-brushes and currycombs were kept, there stood hollowed turnips with candles burning within. A multitude of glow-worms lay among the flowers and leaves on the walls, and gave out their clear green light, tiny and fairy.

One part of the stable was screened off with a leafy curtain and from behind it came muffled laughter, high squeals, and subdued whispers. The curtain scarcely reached the ground and Sam Pig could see little black feet jumping up and down behind it.

The horses were in the stalls, and these were the best seats of all, for of course it was their theatre. Although their backs were to the stage their long heads were turned and their brown eyes gazed in mild surprise. On the partitions of the stalls, perched on the curving oak ledges, were red and white hens, and a couple of cocks splendid in burnished feathers and glittering spurs. They were in the gallery. They were noisy creatures and never ceased pushing and chattering, crowing and cackling even in the most pathetic moment when the heroine lost her slipper.

The body of the stable was occupied by Sally the mare, by the farm pigs, the young calves, and a dozen or more sheep and lambs. The sheep were huddled together looking rather frightened, but the sheep-dog reassured them.

'It's only pretence,' said he, and everybody told everyone else. 'It's only pretence.'

Badger modestly led the way to the back of the stable but the farmyard animals gave up their seats at the front. The door was closed, so that even the moon could not look at the curious scene. Somebody blew out the lamp in the roof, and then the stable was lighted only by the turnip candles and the glow-worms, but a faint gleam came from behind that magical curtain of leaves upon which all eyes were fixed.

The Alderney cow shook her head so that her bell tinkled. Sally the mare twitched the curtain aside, and nibbled a few leaves in her excitement.

Everybody cried 'Oh-o-o-o-o-o!'

There were the seven little pigs from the pig-cote, dressed as fairies, in pink skirts with wreaths of rosebuds round their pink ears. They danced on their nimble black toes, and swung their ballet skirts. They pirouetted until the hens cried out to them.

'Stop a minute! It makes us giddy to watch you!'

'Hush,' said Badger indignantly. 'Hush! No talking!' and the hens stopped clucking for a whole minute and stared down at Badger's black-and-white head.

A band of music makers played in a corner. There was a lamb with a shepherd's pipe, and a Scottish terrier with bagpipes and a kitten with a drum.

'Come along, Sam, and join us,' they beckoned, and Sam stepped shyly through the little dancing pigs who never stopped whirling. He tuned his fiddle and sat down in the corner. Soon he was sawing with might and main, trying to keep time with the squealing of the Scottie's bagpipes, the fluting of the lamb's pipe and the drumming of the little cat.

The farmyard pigs sang their own shrill songs, and the audience joined in the choruses of 'John Barleycorn' and 'A Frog he would a-wooing go'.

They gave an acrobatic display and leaped through hoops of leafy willow on to Sally's broad back. They bowed and bowed again and then the curtain was drawn. It was the interval.

The mother of the dancing pigs handed round refreshments, elderberry wine, and cowslip ale, and cakes of herbs and bunches of hay.

They were all eating and drinking when the Alderney rang her bell. The mare twitched the curtain back, and the lantern went out. Quickly they stuffed their cakes in their mouths and hid their drinking-mugs in the ivy. There was now to be acted the famous play of Cinderella and her straw slipper.

The smallest pig sat in rags by the empty fire-place, and the fine sisters went off to the ball, flaunting their long skirts and their pheasant feathers.

In came a pair of rats drawing a pumpkin across the stable floor. There was such a rustle and flutter among the cocks who wanted to fly down and attack them, such a hiss from the cat, and such a growl

from the Scottie, Badger had to stand up and quieten them.

'It's all pretence,' said he, and they echoed 'Pretence', and were quiet.

The Fairy Godmother waved her wand, and Cinderella's rags fell off. Behold! She was a pink-skirted pigling! Away she went to the ball, riding on the pumpkin, trundling herself along the floor with her little hooves which were covered with shoes of yellow straw.

The next scene was the ballroom, where everyone in the stable danced. Badger danced the polka with the Scottie, and Ann Pig turned with a lamb. Little Sam Pig was chosen by Cinderella herself and he was in great confusion as he tripped and skipped and stumbled over her straw slippers. But the stable clock struck twelve, and Cinderella ran away. Sam tried to hold her but she escaped and hid in a corner out of sight. One of the slippers lay on the floor. Sam Pig picked it up and put it in his pocket.

'Sam Pig! Sam Pig!' called the sow. 'You must go round the theatre and see whose foot is small enough to fit into the little straw slipper.'

'But I know!' answered Sam quickly. 'It belongs to the little Cinderella pig.'

'Hist! Do what I tell you! This is a theatre and it's all pretence,' said the sow sternly. So Sam walked round with the little straw slipper, and everybody tried it on. The mare held out her great hoof, the Alderney held up her delicate foot. The sheep held up their little hooves, and the hens clucked and fussed and stretched out their long thin toes. Little Ann Pig got the slipper on and tried to keep it, but Sam refused to give it up.

'It's not yours, Ann,' he whispered crossly.

Even Badger held out his hairy pad, but Sam pushed it aside.

'I told you so! I told you so! It isn't yours and you can't have it. It belongs to that nice little Cinderella pig, and I don't know where she is.'

He pushed the ugly sisters aside, and there, hiding among the besoms and harness and horse-rugs was little Cinderella. She held out a neat little hoof and Sam Pig dragged the straw slipper upon it. It fitted like a glove!

'Hurrah!' they all cried. 'The Princess is found.' As for Sam, he was so excited he leaned towards her and gave her a kiss. You remember the old

woman in the wood who kissed him? Sam never forgot that nice feeling. Now he kissed Cinderella.

'Hurrah!' cried everybody. 'Hurrah! The Prince has kissed Cinderella.'

'But it's all pretence,' they told one another.

The stable door flew open, and they all flocked out into the cool night air. The sheep scampered away to the pasture, the Alderney walked sedately to the field. The pigs hastened to the pig-cote and nestled together in the shelter of their little home. The cocks and hens scurried back to the hen-place,

escorted by the Scottie. The Fox was staring over the wall wondering what was happening that mid-summer night, but he turned aside when he saw Hamish the Scottie. The cat came out last, and she climbed up on the stable roof.

Brock and the four pigs trundled over the fields to their little home, chattering softly of all they had seen.

'So that's a theatre!' said Brock. 'It was grand! And you, Sam Pig, were the Prince!'

Sam said nothing. All his thoughts were on the little pigling called Cinderella whom he had kissed by the light of the turnip lanterns.

'But it's all pretence,' murmured Ann, and the others echoed, 'Yes. All pretence.'